WHEN I WAS A GIRL,
I USED TO SCREAM AND SHOUT . . .

WHEN I WAS A GIRL, I USED TO SCREAM AND SHOUT . . .

SHARMAN MACDONALD

faber and faber

LONDON · BOSTON

in association with
the Bush Theatre

First published in 1985
by Faber and Faber Limited
3 Queen Square London WC1N 3AU

Photoset by Wilmaset Birkenhead Merseyside
Printed in Great Britain by
Whitstable Litho Ltd Whitstable Kent

British Library Cataloguing in Publication data

Macdonald, Sharman
When I was a girl I used to scream and shout
I. Title
823'.914 [F]   PR6063.A169/

ISBN 0–571–13725–3

CHARACTERS

59 MORAG, the mother

32 FIONA, the daughter

32 VARI, the friend

EWAN, the boyfriend

The play takes place on a rocky beach on the east coast of Scotland. The set is on two levels. Above is part of a prom, a street light and a railing. Below, a tunnel leads through the façade of the prom to the rocks. Cut into the rocks is a small swimming pool about 4 feet square and waist-height.

When I was a Girl I Used to Scream and Shout . . . was first performed at the Bush Theatre, London, in November 1984. The cast was as follows:

MORAG 59	Sheila Reid
FIONA 32	Eleanor David
VARI 32	Celia Imrie
EWAN	John Gordon Sinclair

Directed by	Simon Stokes
Designed by	Robin Don
Music	Richard Brown
Lighting	Paul Denby

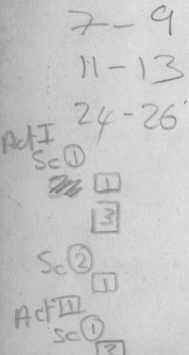

7 – 9
11 – 13
24 – 26
Act I
Sc ①
▦ 1
3
Sc ② 1
Act II
Sc ① 3

Sc ② 1

Sc ③ 5

ACT ONE

SCENE I

1983
The beach.
FIONA *is lying on a towel in a bikini, sunbathing.* MORAG *is sitting
on a travelling rug surrounded by bags.*

MORAG: I'm not dressed up. I bought this years ago. Marks and
    Spencer's. It's a cheap summer dress. It's a nice dress, but
    it's only cheap. You feel the material. Come on over here
    and have a feel of this.
    (FIONA *gets up.*)
    Away and don't bother your head. I wouldn't dress up to
    come down on a beach. I know beaches. All right, these are
    new. I bought a new pair of sandals to come away for the
    weekend. What's wrong with that? It's my own wee treat.
    I'm generous enough with you. I like to look nice. What's
    wrong with that? I've been well groomed all my life. I'll not
    stop now. Not even for you. I'll be smart if I want, but as
    for dressed up . . . What's wrong with you?
FIONA: I said, 'You're all dressed up.' I was smiling.
MORAG: I brought you on this weekend.
FIONA: I'm very grateful.
MORAG: I wanted to see my roses.
FIONA: They're not your roses.
MORAG: I planted them. I tended them. I loved them. But for
    me there'd be no roses. That house can change hands
    umpteen times. Those roses are my roses.
FIONA: All right they're . . .
MORAG: A wee holiday.
FIONA: Mum . . .
MORAG: You can say, 'You're all dressed up' or you can say,
    'You're all dressed up.'
FIONA: You look very smart.
MORAG: We could have a nice time together. A nice quiet
    time.

7

FIONA: The colour suits you.

MORAG: Horse dung, cow dung. I manured those roses with my own hands. All 200 of them. That display is mine.

FIONA: It's beautiful.

MORAG: I thought a nice weekend back here. I've something for you.

FIONA: You shouldn't go on spending money.

MORAG: I mean if you'd said, 'You're all dressed up.'

FIONA: It's a nice dress.

MORAG: No man, no child, no money. I don't like to see you like this.

FIONA: I'm not that bad.

MORAG: I want to bring the brightness back to your eyes. Here. Come here. Come and see.

(*She brings out a coral necklace.* FIONA *gets up and goes to the travelling rug.*)

FIONA: These rocks are burning.

MORAG: Come on to the travelling rug.

FIONA: I'm fine.

MORAG: You'll burn your bum.

FIONA: I'm all right.

MORAG: Oh, well then. Here. This was yours when you were wee. I had a new clasp put on it. It's coral. Here.

(*She fastens it round* FIONA*'s neck and hands her a mirror.*)

What do you think? Of course it's right in the fashion. You get some colour in your skin.

FIONA: It's lovely.

MORAG: You need a man to give you gold. A gold chain lying with that. You've fine skin. Takes me back. That lying round your neck. Do you want a cup of coffee? I've plenty coffee.

FIONA: No.

MORAG: All those years ago and that lying round your chubby wee neck. Fatty, fatty, fatty but awful bonny. I'm going to have some. (*Pours.*) See that necklace. I was keeping that for my first grandchild.

FIONA: You've got a grandchild.

MORAG: That doesn't count.

8

FIONA: Don't be daft.

MORAG: I never held him. I never saw him. I mean a proper child. Of my body. Of your body. You're 32, Fiona. A wee head to hold in my hand. A wee head, Fiona. A wee head to hold in my hand.

FIONA: Did you bring me here for this?

MORAG: You're not showing your age.

FIONA: Did you?

MORAG: You'll burn your bum on those rocks.

FIONA: Am I to have a whole weekend of this?

MORAG: Your Auntie Nellie had the menopause at 30. Are you going to tell me you're happy? You've not even got a man. Come on to the rug.

FIONA: No.

MORAG: Every woman needs to have a child. I remember the day I could wear necklaces. You've my neck. I had a good neck. When I was 32, you were 5. A woman's body is a clock that runs down very rapidly. You don't need me to tell you that.

FIONA: You survived without a man.

MORAG: Did I? I'm here, that's all you can say. I've loved you all your life, Fiona. No matter what you've done. A wee child to hold in my arms. From your body. From my body. A wee child at my knee.

(*A voice from inside the swimming pool –*)

VARI: Hey.

FIONA: Christ.

MORAG: I told her you'd be here.

FIONA: Thanks.

MORAG: Away on over with you.

(FIONA *goes over to the pool.*)

1955
The bedroom.

VARI: Willie games?

FIONA: She'll see.

VARI: Not down here.

FIONA: Pencils?

VARI: Pencils.

(*She holds up two.*)

FIONA: Pram covers?

VARI: Two fluffy ones with bunny rabbits.

FIONA: Excellent.

VARI: Willie games?

FIONA: Yes.

VARI: You come in.

FIONA: (*Jumps in.*) You first.

VARI: I was walking along the road, doctor, and I suddenly realized it wasn't there. I've only got a hole. My penis must have dropped off. Can you help me?

FIONA: It'll be very sore.

VARI: I need my penis back, doctor.

FIONA: There's been a great demand this morning. You can have a red penis or a blue penis.

VARI: Blue, please.

FIONA: Lie down.

VARI: Can you find the hole?

FIONA: It's huge. This'll hurt. You say, 'Ouch.'

VARI: Ouch.

FIONA: That's the operation over.

VARI: You've kind hands, doctor.

FIONA: Thank you.

VARI: I'll need a bandage.

FIONA: I've a nice fluffy one here.

VARI: I like rabbits.

FIONA: There.

VARI: Oh, doctor, will my new penis take?

FIONA: We'll know that tomorrow.

VARI: Now you.

FIONA: Oh, doctor, I kept wetting the bed and my Mummy said if I didn't stop she'd cut it off. Well, I didn't stop so she did cut it off and it hurt a lot, a lot, a lot. Now I don't wet the bed any more can I have a new penis, please?

VARI: You're very lucky I've got one left.

FIONA: What colour is it?

VARI: Red.

FIONA: That'll do nicely, thank you.

VARI: Lie down.

FIONA: I'm not playing.

VARI: I did, you have to.

FIONA: I don't want a pencil stuck up me.

VARI: It's a penis and I've got one stuck up me. And if it takes I'll be a boy and you won't.

(FIONA *gets out of the pool.* VARI *follows.*)

1983
The beach.

FIONA: You were a bloody Queen's Guide. Badges crawling up your arms. The Duke of Edinburgh skulking at your elbow. You made me sick. Always making lemon curd and doing the dusting. You told me there was no Santa Claus. I was sucking a gobstopper. I had just started it. I swallowed it whole. It yo-yo-ed up and down inside me for days. Cause as soon as you said it I knew it was true. There's no Santa Claus.

VARI: So what?

FIONA: Waste of a good gobstopper.

MORAG: What's that bumfle under your skirt, Vari?

VARI: Just keeping warm, Auntie Morag.

MORAG: Never let yourself go, Vari. No matter how tired you are. No matter how depressed you are you can always have your hair nice and your clothes well brushed. And a bit of lipstick won't break the bank. If your lips look like they'll take a kiss things won't go far wrong. You've put on weight.

VARI: I'm always hungry.

MORAG: How many is it now?

VARI: Three.

MORAG: What age?

VARI: Four, 3 and 8 months.

MORAG: I've something for them. I've three silver bracelets here. They used to be Fiona's. Silver's awful pretty on a baby's skin. You take these. Fiona always had a silver bracelet. I was keeping these for my first grandchild but

II

we're out of luck. Fiona's Auntie Nellie, well, her Great Auntie, my Auntie that was, Auntie Nellie had the menopause at 30.

FIONA: I had a baby.

MORAG: At least we know you're fertile.

VARI: They're lovely. The girls'll be delighted. Thank you very much.

MORAG: You've not been a mother. You're a sad woman. Look at your eyes.

VARI: Look at mine, Auntie Morag, I don't get a night's sleep.

MORAG: I've a nice cup of tea here. 'The old Bohea,' Fiona's Great Aunt Jean used to say. Her that was Auntie Nellie's sister.

FIONA: The bracelets dug into my arm.

MORAG: When you come down to the beach you've got to be prepared. I bring coffee, tea, sandwiches and cake. And of course the odd bit of fruit and a biscuit or two. I know beaches.

(*She begins to lay out a picnic.*)

VARI: What have you come here for?

MORAG: All the sandwiches are on brown bread. I insist on that. I'm not a faddy eater but brown bread is a must in my eyes. Of course Fiona's a vegetarian. So difficult at the hotel.

FIONA: We came because she wanted to.

MORAG: And she doesn't like eggs.

VARI: What for?

MORAG: There's so much nonsense talked about food. Health this and whole that. Fiona's Great Auntie Nellie lived till she was 90 and her favourite food was rare steak covered in cream. Will you have a corned-beef sandwich?

VARI: Thank you.

MORAG: Of course she lost all her hair with the menopause. I've cheese and tomato for you. Apart from that she was healthy.

FIONA: No, thank you.

MORAG: You take it. I'll not see you scraggy. I can count your ribs. A man likes a bit of flesh to puddle his fingers in. Vari's three children are the living proof of that. Hours you'd spend in that bedroom. I could always trust you two to play together. Not like boys. Always with their hands on their dirty wee things. Do you take sugar?

VARI: Two, please.

MORAG: Another sandwich?

VARI: Yes, please.

MORAG: Have you thought of joining the Weight Watchers?

VARI: I'm always like this when I'm feeding.

MORAG: Three children. You'll never be lonely. Be a good daughter to your mother and your children'll do good by you. Eat your sandwich, Fiona, you look drawn.

FIONA: You don't look well, Fiona. We're none of us getting any younger, Fiona. You've bags under your eyes, you've wrinkles in your forehead, your wee bit breasts are sagging. Child, menopause, child. It's a mother's place to worry. What else am I going to do? I've all my eggs in the one basket. I didn't want to come back here. What do you want to come back here for?

MORAG: It was a good place to live.

FIONA: If you've something to say to me will you not just say it?

MORAG: I've lived without a man these past seventeen years. I'm lonely. I want a grandchild.

(Silence.)

VARI: These are lovely sandwiches.

MORAG: I'd say that was my right.

FIONA: It is not.

MORAG: What did I give birth to you for?

VARI: Could I maybe have another cup of tea?

MORAG: Come on to the rug, you'll burn your bum.

(FIONA goes to the pool and gets in. VARI follows.)

1959
The bathroom.

VARI: Do you know where babies come from?

FIONA: Up your Auntie Mary. Down the plug-hole.

VARI: Do you know how they get in there?

FIONA: A woman has a period and a man has a period, sort of, and if they coincide and they happen to be touching, if

13

they're married and they're in bed together then the woman gets a baby.

VARI: How do you know that?

FIONA: I just do.

VARI: See when you get your doings you have to be very careful. I mean if a man touches you then, even if a finger of a man touches you, you might get pregnant.

FIONA: My Daddy?

VARI: You'll have to keep him off.

FIONA: Girls don't get pregnant to their fathers.

VARI: Girls are careful. After you've got your doings every time you have a big job, you know the hard kind you have to press out, you mind and look behind you. There might be a baby swimming about there down the bog in amongst the jobbies. So don't pull the flush too quick.

FIONA: What else am I going to do with it?

VARI: You'd have to love it and take care of it.

FIONA: I'm not putting my hand down there to fish it out.

VARI: Your mum likes babies.

FIONA: She'd be cross. She's very bad tempered, my mum. She'd think I'd been careless.

VARI: You'd just have to break it to her gently.

FIONA: I think I'd rather pull the flush.

VARI: You're disgusting.

FIONA: Well, what would you do?

VARI: My mum says always to remember that whatever I do she'd always love me so never be afraid to tell her anything cause she'd take care of me.

FIONA: My mum said that too.

VARI: They're talking about babies.

FIONA: I still think they'd be cross.

VARI: You've got hairs.

FIONA: Where?

VARI: Down there. Look.

FIONA: Oh, yes. They're nice.

VARI: I haven't got any.

FIONA: There's six. Daddy, Daddy.

(VARI *puts her hand over* FIONA's *mouth*.)

VARI: Let me get out first.

FIONA: Daddy, Daddy, Daddy, Daddy, Daddy, Daddy.

(MORAG *jumps up and runs over.*)

MORAG: What is it? What is it?

FIONA: I've got hair. I've got six hairs. Go and get Daddy.

MORAG: I thought you'd gone down the plug-hole. The fuss.

FIONA: Get Daddy. Get Daddy.

MORAG: What do you want him for?

FIONA: I want him to see. Have I got breasts? Look, I've got bumps. Go and get Daddy.

MORAG: You can't have your father in the bathroom.

FIONA: Why not?

MORAG: You're very nearly a young lady.

FIONA: He'd like to see my hairs.

MORAG: You must always have your clothes on when you see your father.

FIONA: But my hairs.

MORAG: I'll tell him.

FIONA: You haven't looked.

MORAG: Very nice.

FIONA: They're black. Did you see? Did you? Soon it'll be a forest. That'll be nice. Dorothy hasn't got hair and she's older than me. She says she used to have breasts but they've gone down to get more skin so that they can come back up again.

MORAG: You're to stop asking your father to tickle your tummy on a Saturday morning.

FIONA: He likes it.

MORAG: You'll have your doings soon. You'll be a young lady. That'll make Gran proud. Daddies don't tickle the tummies of young ladies.

FIONA: You've not to tell Gran. Who'll tickle my tummy? I need my tummy tickled. Don't tell Gran. Promise. I don't want to be a young lady.

MORAG: It can be the curse indeed.

FIONA: I've just got hairs. Don't tell. Don't tell anyone. No one's to know. It'll be a secret, you and me. If I get breasts I'll cross my arms and no one'll know.

MORAG: We're not great ones for breasts in our family.

FIONA: If I don't have them no man'll ever want me.

MORAG: I did all right. You're a very pretty girl and don't let anyone tell you other. Now. Out of the bath and straight to bed.

(FIONA *stands up.* MORAG *wraps her in a towel and bustles her to the sunbathing area.* FIONA *lies down.*)

1960

The bedroom.

MORAG: One story, that's all.

FIONA: Two.

MORAG: One, then sleep.

FIONA: Two.

MORAG: We'll see.

FIONA: Please. Please.

MORAG: One.

FIONA: Two.

MORAG: Move over.

(FIONA *wriggles her bum to take up all the towel.*)
Move or I'll go downstairs.

(FIONA *doesn't move.* MORAG *sets off for the tunnel.*)

FIONA: I've moved. Don't go. I've moved. I've moved.

(MORAG *comes back and begins to settle herself beside her daughter on the towel.* FIONA *is wriggling.*)

MORAG: What are you doing?

FIONA: Jigging.

MORAG: Keep still.

FIONA: Why?

MORAG: How jigging?

FIONA: Like this.

MORAG: What's it for?

FIONA: Makes me sleepy.

MORAG: Why?

FIONA: Feels nice.

MORAG: I see.

FIONA: Tell me a story.

MORAG: How nice?

16

FIONA: You know.

MORAG: I'm hoping I don't know. I'm hoping that you're my own good girl. Are you?

FIONA: Yes.

MORAG: I'm glad. Where does it feel nice?

FIONA: Inside.

MORAG: Where inside?

FIONA: Between my legs and up a bit.

MORAG: It's a bad thing you're doing.

FIONA: It makes me sleepy.

MORAG: I couldn't tell Daddy you were doing this.

FIONA: Why?

MORAG: Now you know there's a God upstairs and he looks down and he sees everything you do.

FIONA: I'll only do it in the dark.

MORAG: God can see in the dark. He sees everything and everyone and if he spots wee Fiona jigging in her bed in the dark, do you know what he does? Do you?

FIONA: What does he do?

MORAG: He looks down and he says to himself, 'That wee Fiona's a naughty, naughty girl and I thought she was one of my better efforts. That wee Fiona's jigging. Tttt. Tttt. Tttt,' he goes. And he calls the Recording Angel. And he says to the Recording Angel, 'I put wee Fiona on the earth to make her mummy happy and look at her now. Jigging. Recording Angel,' says God and the Recording Angel says, 'Yes, Lord.' 'Recording Angel,' says God, 'take up your pen' and the Recording Angel, who's always crying for he has a very sad job, takes up his great big feather pen with the sharp point. 'Recording Angel,' says God, 'open up the book and dip the pen.' The Recording Angel opens the big red book that hangs from his waist by a chain and dips his pen in God's great big inkwell. 'Find wee Fiona's name,' says God and he looks down in his infinite kindness to give you one more chance but you're still jigging away down there in the dark and God blushes for the shame of it and the Recording Angel's tears fall all the faster. And God says, 'Put a black mark at wee Fiona's name, she's a

17

disappointment to me' and the Recording Angel puts a big black mark at your name. And do you know what happens if you get enough black marks? Do you, Fiona?

FIONA: No.

MORAG: You don't go to heaven to pick the flowers in God's green meadows when you die. God casts you down. He looks in his big book and he sees all the black marks. He says, 'I don't want wee Fiona here to dirty up my nice heaven' and he sends you down, all the way down to the devil who's like a snake only worse and the devil sticks you on a spit and roasts you in the fires of hell so he can eat you for dinner.

FIONA: Does it hurt?

MORAG: Oh, yes, it hurts a lot.

FIONA: For jigging?

MORAG: That's right.

FIONA: If I stop now do you think God'll say it's all right?

MORAG: I'm sure he'll be very proud of you.

FIONA: I won't do it any more.

MORAG: That's my good girl. Mummy loves you very much. Mummy will always love you whatever you do.

FIONA: What about God?

MORAG: I'll have a word. Good night. Sleep tight. Don't let the bugs bite.

(MORAG *goes.* VARI *comes over surreptitiously from the swimming pool and crouches by* FIONA'S *head.*)

1961

The bedroom.

VARI: She's got it all wrong.

FIONA: What?

VARI: There's no God.

FIONA: Yes, there is.

VARI: No, there isn't.

FIONA: Yes, there is.

VARI: I was right about Santa Claus.

FIONA: Does that mean it's all right to do it?

VARI: No.

FIONA: Why?

VARI: If you do that your husband'll know when you get married and he'll despise you.

FIONA: How will he know? You can't see.

VARI: If you keep doing it you go all hard inside. You go like concrete and he can't get in to get his pleasure. So he knows.

FIONA: Why does he want to get in?

VARI: His penis needs to. It sort of gets up and leads him to the hole and it tries to get in and if it can't the man knows it's your fault and you get divorced. He knows you've been dirty and no man'll live with a dirty lady. He shouldn't be expected to, my mum says.

FIONA: Are you sure his penis goes in?

VARI: I've seen.

FIONA: Oh, well.

VARI: Do you want me to tell you?

FIONA: I think I've had enough for one night.

VARI: What're you lying all scrunched up for?

FIONA: I've got snakes in the bed. They're all round me and I've only got this tiny space to lie in.

VARI: That's not very nice.

FIONA: They're under the bed too and there's bugs on the wall. But there's a gun where the door handle used to be and if I can reach that I'll be all right.

VARI: Did you know your mum and dad were getting divorced?

FIONA: Is there still a Jesus?

VARI: Seems to be proof of that.

FIONA: That's nice.

VARI: Did you hear me?

FIONA: My mum and dad are getting divorced. (*Pause.*) Has she gone all hard inside?

VARI: He's got another woman. Who can blame him, my mum says. Do you believe me?

FIONA: Yes. What about me?

VARI: My mum says you've been a bit of a disappointment. My mum says your father didn't want a child and your mum tricked him to get you. Said it was safe when it wasn't.

FIONA: My mum must love me then.

VARI: Suppose she must. She won't like her man going though, my mum says, it's a terrible stigma.

FIONA: Are you sure about Jesus?

VARI: Oh, yes.

FIONA: Does he live in the sky?

VARI: He's dead.

FIONA: There's not a lot of point in that then.

VARI: What?

FIONA: I thought he might help with my mum and dad.

VARI: No chance.

FIONA: I'm going to sleep now.

VARI: In the dark. I'm scared of the dark.

FIONA: So am I.

VARI: There's bogies in the dark.

FIONA: I know.

VARI: They'll get you.

FIONA: I know.

VARI: We could both get in together, then we'd be all right.

FIONA: What do you mean?

VARI: I could get in with you. You're awful thick sometimes.

FIONA: Why?

VARI: Bogies don't attack you when you're with someone.

FIONA: Why not?

VARI: Never mind why not. They don't, that's all. But if you want the bogies to get you, that's your tough tof.

FIONA: OK then.

VARI: OK then what?

FIONA: Get in.

VARI: I don't know if I want to now.

FIONA: Och, Vari, come on.

VARI: Bogies cling to the wall and drop on your face and they suffocate you. It's a horrible death, my mum says.

FIONA: Gonnie get in?

FIONA: Say 'Please'.

FIONA: Please.

VARI: Move then.

(VARI *gets into the towel bed*.)

Are you sure there's snakes in here?

FIONA: Yes.

VARI: I can't feel them.

FIONA: They're only here for me.

VARI: Right, I'm comfy.

FIONA: Good.

VARI: I've an idea.

FIONA: What?

VARI: Do you want to know what it's like when a man and woman do it?

FIONA: Eh?

VARI: Do you?

FIONA: What, now?

VARI: Why not?

FIONA: How?

VARI: I'll be the man and you be the woman.

FIONA: What do I do?

VARI: Take your jammies off.

FIONA: I will not.

VARI: Shhhhh. Shhhhh. Do you want everyone to hear? It's only sensible to practise. We've got to make it as real as possible. I mean, you don't think they do it with their clothes on, do you?

FIONA: I don't know.

VARI: Well, they don't. It's only sensible. How can his thing go in you if you've got a pair of pyjamas in the way? That's what's known as contraception.

FIONA: Sorry.

VARI: I've got mine off. Hurry up.

FIONA: Ready.

VARI: Right. I'm going to kiss your ear.

FIONA: Why?

VARI: That's what they do. Ready?

FIONA: Yes.

(VARI *kisses* FIONA's *ear*.)

VARI: Right. That's that bit. Was it nice?

FIONA: Yes.

VARI: Now I'm going to kiss your mouth.

FIONA: No.

VARI: I've got to.

FIONA: I don't want you to.

VARI: It won't work if we don't do it properly.

FIONA: I don't like it.

VARI: All right, we'll skip the mouth bit. I'll just get on top of you.

FIONA: No.

VARI: Do you want to practise or not?

FIONA: All right.

VARI: Right. Try to just concentrate, will you. I mean you'd think we were doing something dirty.

FIONA: Sorry.

VARI: Right. (*Gets on top of* FIONA.) How's that? Am I heavy?

FIONA: No. Not really.

VARI: Do I feel nice?

FIONA: I suppose so.

VARI: Don't be so enthusiastic. I mean, I'm the one doing all the work.

FIONA: Sorry.

VARI: Right. I haven't got one so I'll just jig up and down a bit.

FIONA: Jigging.

VARI: What?

FIONA: Stop.

VARI: I don't want to.

FIONA: It's jigging, Vari. God'll see.

VARI: There's no God.

FIONA: It feels like jigging.

VARI: I told you there's no God.

FIONA: Aye. But what if there is?

VARI: What if?

FIONA: He'll look down and he'll see. Get off.

VARI: Not now.

FIONA: Get off.

VARI: Do you mean it?

FIONA: I mean it. I mean it. Get off.

VARI: I won't be your best friend any more.

FIONA: Sorry.

VARI: So am I.

FIONA: Will you be able to sleep?

VARI: I can always sleep.

FIONA: I really am awful sorry.

VARI: I'll just find someone else to practise with and you'll feel an awful idiot when you have to do it for real and you don't know how.

FIONA: Who will you find?

VARI: I'm not telling.

FIONA: Go on.

VARI: You're just like your mum. My mum says you can't hold back on a man. You won't keep a man either.

FIONA: My mum says you've got to keep your kisses for the man you love and if you don't you're cheap and you didn't say there wasn't a devil and the devil gets you for jigging and that's a well-known fact and I don't care what you say we were jigging. I've got enough to contend with with bugs and bogies, never mind asking the devil to pay a visit too. Now you go home. I've a busy night ahead of me. I've 345 snakes in this bed and I've got to kill them all by morning and I haven't even reached the gun yet.

VARI: You're a prude, Fiona McBridie.

FIONA: Go away.

VARI: You just see if I care. (*Half goes.*) You're going to be half an orphan as good as and nobody'll like you any more. (*Blackout.*)

23

SCENE 2

1983
The beach. Bright sunlight.
MORAG *is on the rug.* FIONA *is drying herself.*

FIONA: Well?

MORAG: Is it your business?

FIONA: He was my dad. You're my mother.

MORAG: You've never asked before.

FIONA: I was very young when he went.

MORAG: That's about the sum of it.

FIONA: What?

MORAG: When your father left I was 37. I was very grateful to
him that I wasn't 40. And that was my chief emotion. I
knew he was going to go. All I prayed was that he'd not
hang it out. It's a different thing trying to get another man
at 40. At 37 I even had another baby in me. Maybe. If some
man hurried up. got on with it

FIONA: Why didn't you leave him?

MORAG: I loved him but if he went I didn't want to spend the
rest of my life without a man. I like men. Not sex, you
understand. That's dirty. Your father was like an elephant,
if he got it once in ten years he could consider himself
lucky. So he went. I could never see anything in it. With
the telly now I can see I must have been wrong. I mean,
there wouldn't be such a fuss if there was nothing in it.

FIONA: That's sad.

MORAG: Not in the least. You're 32 and you've not got a child.
That's sad.

FIONA: I don't want one.

MORAG: Rubbish.

FIONA: I don't

MORAG: Every woman wants a child.

FIONA: Not me.

MORAG: It's not as if your career's a success.

24

FIONA: It might be.

MORAG: I'm paying for this holiday.

FIONA: I only came to keep you company.

MORAG: I only came because you were looking so awful I thought you'd never get a man and that's all the thanks I get.

FIONA: I've got several men.

MORAG: Don't be dirty.

FIONA: Well, I have.

MORAG: Where are they then? I don't see them.

FIONA: They sure as hell aren't on the east coast of Scotland having a quiet weekend with my mother, being intruded on by a best friend I haven't seen for seventeen years.

MORAG: Are you a lesbian? (*Pause.*) Don't look at me like that. I'm only asking.

FIONA: I didn't even know you knew the word.

MORAG: Don't be silly. My own sister was one, of course I know the word.

FIONA: Who?

MORAG: Jane.

FIONA: Jane's married.

MORAG: Oh, aye, she did eventually but that was after.

FIONA: What?

MORAG: You haven't answered me.

FIONA: What?

MORAG: Are you a lesbian?

FIONA: I'm not going to answer you.

MORAG: I won't tell you about your Aunt Jane.

FIONA: Stuff you then.

MORAG: Don't talk to your mother like that. It was a civilized question. I expect a civilized answer.

FIONA: No, I'm not a lesbian, I just don't want a baby. Now, what about Auntie Jane?

MORAG: I thought I'd have known about it. I mean you've ruined my life with your other problems. I suppose you'd have found some way to let me know about that. You know what I'm talking about.

(*Pause.*)

FIONA: Tell me about Auntie Jane.

MORAG: Of course your grandmother was appalled, sort of.

FIONA: Did she know?

MORAG: They did it under her roof. I always thought that was most unwise. Your grandmother threw them out, told them to book into a hotel but she didn't want the sounds of their pleasure coming through her bedroom ceiling. It was bad enough with a man. It was an ATS sergeant. Your Auntie Jane was between 20 and 30 and single in the war years so she got conscripted. She'd have gone anyway. She liked the uniform and she was awful patriotic. That's why she emigrated to South Africa and not because of the scandal as some thought.

FIONA: What scandal?

MORAG: It was whispered up and down our street. The ATS sergeant was crop-haired. She had a low voice and a flat chest. She and Jane walked around arm in arm. The ATS sergeant was never out of uniform and Jane had always had a softness for frills. It was awful obvious. But that was when the bombs were falling on Clydebank and Glasgow. Your grandmother relented. she thought her children should have their pleasure before a bomb got them. Whatever their pleasure might be. She didn't insist they left the house, just moved them to another bedroom so she didn't have to listen. Then they were next to me so that's how I knew for certain. I thought it might run in the family.

FIONA: What have we come here for?

MORAG: Well, that's a relief. I didn't quite know what kind of a face I was going to put on it if you were.

FIONA: Answer me.

MORAG: What, dear?

FIONA: Why have we come here?

MORAG: For a rest, dear.

1966
The beach.
VARI *runs down the rocks.*

VARI: Five numbers. One, two, three, four, five. One for
    kissing. Two for tongue in the mouth. Three for breast.
    Four for fingers. Five for your hand on him.

FIONA: What's after five?

    (*Pause.*)

VARI: Six.

FIONA: What's number six?

VARI: It goes up to ten.

FIONA: What are the others?

VARI: Don't be dirty.

FIONA: You don't know.

VARI: How far have you gone?

FIONA: How far have you gone?

VARI: You first.

FIONA: No, you.

VARI: I asked you first.

FIONA: I asked you second.

VARI: Scaredy cat. I won't tell. I know. You're a whore. You've
    been to ten and back again. Only whores go to ten.

FIONA: Don't be silly.

VARI: Apart from mothers.

FIONA: What's number four?

VARI: His fingers up you.

    (*Silence.*)

    You're dirty.

FIONA: I didn't say I had, I just asked what it was.

    (*Silence.*)

    What do his fingers do up you?

VARI: Don't be daft.

FIONA: What do they do?

VARI: You know.

FIONA: What?

VARI: Wiggle about a bit.

FIONA: What does it feel like?

VARI: Haven't you ever . . . ? You know.

FIONA: What?

VARI: Done it to yourself.

FIONA: No. Should I? Is it nice?

27

VARI: It's all right.

FIONA: Is it nice when he does it?

VARI: Promise you won't tell.

FIONA: Promise.

VARI: Promise.

FIONA: Promise.

VARI: I've only done it once.

FIONA: When?

VARI: I'm telling you. Shut up. It was here. Up by the tunnel. Last Saturday. I was allowed out to eleven so . . .

FIONA: Ten o'clock, me.

VARI: Do you want to hear? We got down here and we were holding hands and that was a bit boring. I mean he's not a great conversationalist.

FIONA: He's got lovely legs. And a black PVC raincoat.

VARI: We sat on that. It was warm last Saturday.

FIONA: Could you smell the shit from the sewers? I never think that's very romantic. What's wrong?

VARI: I'm just thinking I'm not going to tell you.

FIONA: I'm sorry.

VARI: You're always sticking your oar in.

FIONA: What did he stick?

(*They giggle and they giggle.*)

VARI: Anyway he kissed me. You know nice little nibbling ones not the great wet open-mouthed kind you get from some of them. Nice little nibbling things on the corner of my mouth and just down a bit. Then he put his tongue in my mouth and that got a bit boring so I took his hand and put it on my breast. My right breast, I think it was. He seemed to like that though he didn't do much. Then that got a bit boring so I put my hand on his thing. Don't look like that. There comes a time when you've got to, you know, take things into your own hands. So I did. I mean I'd never seen one except on statues. Anyway tit for tat. He was groping away so why shouldn't I? It was all hard. I suppose I should have expected that but it was an awful shock. I sort of rubbed away a bit. Then he did it. He got it out. He undid his trousers and out it came.

28

(*Pause.*)

FIONA: Well?

VARI: It was very big. How does that ever fit into you? It was all sort of stretched and a bit purple. Though I couldn't see very well. It seemed rude to stop and stare. I mean if you've got something like that I don't suppose you really want it looked at. He didn't. Cause he got on top of me. He pushed me over. He pulled up my skirt. He stuck his fingers up inside my pants and inside me. Then he rubbed a bit, you know, himself up and down on me. Then he sort of gasped and stopped. There was this great wet patch on my skirt when I got up. I told my mum I'd dropped my ice-cream, you know, old-fashioned vanilla. Say something. Go on. You think I'm dirty.

FIONA: I don't.

VARI: You do.

FIONA: I was just wondering what number it was that you got to.

(EWAN, *long-legged and in black PVC, comes to the mouth of the tunnel.*)

VARI: Look.

FIONA: It's him.

VARI: Go on, he knows what to do. You try him.

FIONA: Me?

VARI: You like his legs.

FIONA: Another time.

VARI: Sure.

FIONA: He's waving to you.

VARI: There was this great lump of rock sticking in my back. I've got a bruise.

(VARI *goes off through the tunnel with* EWAN.)

1966

The bathroom.

MORAG: (*Calling from the bath*) Bring me my clothes and get yourself in here. I'll not call again.

FIONA: Here.

MORAG: Sit down, I want a word.

FIONA: (*Sits gingerly.*) What?

MORAG: I'm 42 years old.

FIONA: Did I not remember your birthday?

MORAG: Don't be daft. You don't look very comfortable.

FIONA: I'm all right. What do you want?

MORAG: Your father left five years ago.

FIONA: I know that.

(*She shifts, stands up, smooths her skirt at the back.*)

MORAG: Will you keep still, I'm trying to talk to you. Here, hold the towel, I'm getting out.

(*She gets out. She's in a bathing suit. She drapes the towel.*) Here, look at me. I'm no half bad. I've always had a good figure, no one can deny me that. I've done my exercises through morning and night. My stomach's like a board. No baggy skin and I never had any breasts so you won't see them sagging. If you cut off my head you'd think I was 19. Pity about my head. If I had money I'd go straight to a plastic surgeon. A wee pull here, a stretch there. You've got St Vitus's dance.

FIONA: You're a very attractive woman.

MORAG: Thank you, Fiona. Grooming. Always be smart. Even if you're poor your clothes can be well brushed. You've not been still since you came in here.

FIONA: Sorry.

MORAG: We've always had a good relationship, you and me. Well? We have, haven't we?

FIONA: Yes.

MORAG: So. As I say, your father left five years ago.

FIONA: Yes.

MORAG: Oh, Fiona, I've found a man. I'm in love. I never really thought it would happen to me. I say I found him. He really found me. I feel 17. I'm happy. I'm going to ask him to the house and I wanted very humbly to ask your permission. I want him to come to dinner and I wanted you to meet him. What do you say?

FIONA: I've run out of sanitary towels.

MORAG: Pardon?

FIONA: I'm on the last one in the house and that's nearly through. I'm going to get blood on my skirt.

MORAG: Go and buy some.

FIONA: You didn't order them from the Co-op.

MORAG: I forgot.

FIONA: You always order them with the messages.

MORAG: My mind wasn't on it. Can he come to dinner?

FIONA: What am I going to do?

MORAG: Put your coat on. Get some at the corner shop.

FIONA: No.

MORAG: Don't be daft. You can't not have sanitary towels. That's dirty.

FIONA: Have you slept with him?

MORAG: There's money in my purse.

FIONA: I can't.

MORAG: Don't be stupid.

FIONA: There's a man in the corner shop.

MORAG: Men know women have periods.

FIONA: But he'll know it's actually coming out of me now. I'll be standing there bleeding in his shop and he'll know.

MORAG: Wait for the woman to come out from the back.

FIONA: You go.

MORAG: I will not.

FIONA: You're the one who forgot.

MORAG: You're the one who's bleeding.

FIONA: But I'm not a woman.

MORAG: Get the money from my purse and get along to that shop before you spoil your nice clothes.

FIONA: No.

MORAG: It'll be closed soon and then where'll you be?

FIONA: Bloody.

MORAG: You watch your tongue.

FIONA: I'm not going. You're my mother. You're supposed to take care of me.

MORAG: You'll feel the back of my hand.

FIONA: I won't go. You forgot. You forgot.

MORAG: (Dressing) I saw you when you were born. Two hours I was in labour with you and you ripped me right up to my

31

bum. You came out from between my legs and your eyes were open. You knew exactly what you'd done. The midwife held you up. You looked right at me. You didn't cry. No, madam. Not you. You gave me look for look. I didn't like you then and I don't like you now. Do you hear me, Fiona? Are you listening, Fiona? I don't like you. Nasty little black thing you were. You had hair to your shoulders and two front teeth. You wouldn't suck. I tried to feed you. I did everything that was proper. You'd take nothing from me. Your father took you. He dandled you and petted you. You had eyes for him all right. Well, he's not here now. You won't find him down at the corner shop buying your sanitary towels. I took care of you. I clothed you and washed you and you had your fair share of cuddles. Sometimes I even quite liked you. Though you've gone your own way. You smoke, don't you? Don't you look at me like that. You walk back from that school every day, save the bus money for cigarettes. I know you do. I've seen you. I've not said. I've not said all I know about you. You sat on your father's knee, you clapped his head, you could get anything you wanted. You thought you could. You thought you could. You're still just a wee girl. Hanging round the prom on a Sunday teatime. I've seen you. Hanging round the boys. I've seen you, butter wouldn't melt in your mouth with your Sunday morning piety fresh on you and a smell of smoke on your breath. I've seen you looking at them. Sleekit smile on your face. You know it all. Well, do you, my girl? Do you know it all? You live in my house and in my house you do as I say and if anything happens to you with your sly ways you'll not stay in my house. You'll be out the door and you'll not come back. What you ask for you get. Now go and buy your sanitary towels.

(*Silence.*)

I'm sorry. I love you. I'll always love you. I'm just out of the bath, Fiona. Are you asking me to catch my death?

FIONA: You've gone to bed with him.

MORAG: I'll not have you spreading blood on my furniture.

FIONA: You've let him touch you.

MORAG: Get the sanitary towels.

FIONA: It's a sin what you've done.

MORAG: Get to that shop.

FIONA: You're a sinner.

MORAG: Get.

FIONA: You're a whore.

(MORAG *hits* FIONA *hard.* MORAG *goes to the towel. She picks up a coat and goes down the tunnel.*)

1966
The beach.

VARI: (*Popping up*) Why did you not just go?

FIONA: It's dark.

VARI: So what?

FIONA: I'm scared of the dark.

VARI: If she gets a cold where'll you be?

FIONA: I don't care.

VARI: She wants to go away.

FIONA: Who?

VARI: Auntie Morag.

FIONA: Why?

VARI: Her man's got a job abroad. He's in oil. He's got to go to some Arab country or other. He wants her to go with him and she wants to go.

FIONA: She does not.

VARI: She does so.

FIONA: What about me?

VARI: You're not liable to get to university via the Trucial States so she asked my mum if you could live with us, as a paying guest, seeing as we're friends.

FIONA: I don't want to live with you.

VARI: Why not?

FIONA: I want to live in my own house with my own mother. She can't go pissing off. She's responsible for me. She loves me.

VARI: She loves her man.

FIONA: When did she talk to your mum?

33

VARI: The day before yesterday.

FIONA: Why didn't she tell me first?

VARI: She guessed how well you'd take it.

FIONA: I'll live with my dad. He loves me.

VARI: Your dad's got three wee kids of his own.

FIONA: I'm his own.

VARI: It's not an option.

FIONA: My dad loves me.

VARI: Your mum's checked it out. He doesn't want you. He said you could go for the odd weekend. You're not that easy to get on with. Adolescents never are.

FIONA: Where are the Trucial States?

VARI: On the Persian Gulf.

FIONA: There's oil here.

VARI: It's hotter over there and you don't have to live in the middle of the sea.

FIONA: She's a whore.

VARI: That's what my mum says. My mum says that them that come to it late are insatiable.

FIONA: It's my dad's bed.

VARI: She doesn't want to live on her own for the rest of her life. My mum's jealous. I don't think sex with my dad's a party.

FIONA: I'm not going to let her go.

VARI: You can't stop her.

FIONA: I can.

VARI: How?

FIONA: I'll stop her.

1983

The beach.

MORAG: Oh, my God, would you look at that?

FIONA: It's a jellyfish.

VARI: Oh, God.

FIONA: It's not doing you any harm.

MORAG: I'll be the judge of that.

VARI: It's oozing, Auntie Morag.

MORAG: Get rid of it.

FIONA: They sleep together in our house.

EWAN: Where do you expect them to go?

FIONA: It's disgusting.

EWAN: She's not that old, your mum. Women probably need it as well as men. Your dad left a long time ago.

FIONA: Shut up.

EWAN: It'd do you good.

FIONA: I'm not 16.

EWAN: What about it though?

FIONA: What?

EWAN: I could come to your house when your mum's at work.

FIONA: My bedroom's at the front.

EWAN: That's nice for you. You'll have a sea view.

FIONA: Everyone'll see if I close the curtains during the day.

EWAN: Is that what's stopping you?

FIONA: They'll see you coming in, someone will even if you go round the back and if I close the curtains they'll know exactly what we're doing. The boy across the road hangs his penis out his upstairs window in his bare scuddy. The woman next door warned my mum so that I wouldn't look but he only does it for me so it seems awful rude not to. He's always looking out for me so he can do it. He'd tell. The woman next door's got the police to him three times. She says she's got an interest in my welfare and he's a traffic hazard. He'd tell to get his own back. He thinks it's my fault he does it. You know, for being there. He was born in his house and we moved into ours and my bedroom's really the dining room so I shouldn't be there anyway. That's what he thinks. I'm always getting flashed at.

EWAN: Want a look?

FIONA: Don't be daft.

EWAN: You're very pretty.

FIONA: Thanks.

EWAN: Give us a kiss.

(MORAG *is on the prom.* FIONA *and* EWAN *are necking on the rocks.*)

MORAG: Fiona. Come here. Come here.

FIONA: Oh, Christ.

37

EWAN: Leave this to me. Stay there.

FIONA: I'll have to come.

EWAN: I'll deal with it.

FIONA: All right but I'm coming too.

MORAG: Move yourself, Fiona.

> (*They join* MORAG *above*.)
>
> What do you think you're doing, the pair of you? You're in public.

EWAN: I must apologize, Mrs McBridie, it was entirely my fault.

MORAG: You were both getting your lips wet.

EWAN: At my behest.

MORAG: Indeed. And who are you?

EWAN: Ewan Campbell. I live up the Crescent.

MORAG: Do you?

EWAN: I do.

MORAG: You'll be the one at the bus stop in the uniform of the Academy.

EWAN: I've often admired your roses.

MORAG: Och, away with you. I know fine what you're trying to do. You won't get round me.

EWAN: Will you accept my apologies for kissing your daughter in public?

MORAG: You were half-way down her throat. If that was kissing times have changed.

EWAN: You've changed with them.

MORAG: Have I?

EWAN: May I take your daughter to the cinema?

MORAG: I said she wasn't to go out with a boy till she was 16.

FIONA: Please, Mum.

MORAG: You'll sit in the chummies and smooch all the way through the film.

EWAN: We'll endeavour to give you a good account of the story afterwards.

MORAG: I'll expect you to the house for tea before you go. Don't let me down again, the pair of you. There's plenty of time for that sort of thing when you're older.

FIONA: Your age.

MORAG: Mind your mouth.

EWAN: I'll be seeing you on Saturday then?

FIONA: Yes.

EWAN: Goodbye, Mrs McBridie.

MORAG: Aye.

(EWAN *goes out through the tunnel.*)

I want to talk to you.

FIONA: You were flirting with him.

MORAG: I'd be trying to get off with him right enough.

FIONA: I didn't want him to come to the house.

MORAG: I'm sorry. I thought he was your friend.

FIONA: You can have your man there and we'll be a cosy wee foursome. You can have one on either side and show off your winsome ways. Flutter your eyelashes.

MORAG: You've a cheap tongue.

FIONA: You wanted me.

MORAG: Yes.

FIONA: Is this it?

MORAG: What?

FIONA: You're going away. (*Pause.*) Why didn't you tell me?

MORAG: I couldn't.

FIONA: You're a whore and you're not even brave.

MORAG: Don't speak to me like that.

FIONA: Why didn't you tell me?

MORAG: I want to sell the house and go with him.

FIONA: I won't let you.

MORAG: In two years you'll be at university. I don't want to spend the rest of my life on my own.

FIONA: I might want to go to university here.

MORAG: You'll not want to stay with me.

FIONA: You're supposed to take care of me.

MORAG: If I could take you with me I would.

FIONA: Would you?

MORAG: I love you very much.

FIONA: You don't love me. Love. You love yourself. You love your reflection in a man's eyes. The first man that comes along you abandon me. Fuck you, Mother.

MORAG: Fiona.

FIONA: I don't want him in the house.
  (FIONA *runs down to the beach*.)

1966
The beach.
VARI: What are you going to do? Have you decided?
FIONA: Know any good jokes?
VARI: What?
FIONA: I could do with a laugh.
VARI: What are you going to do?
FIONA: Right, I'll tell you one.
VARI: Is it dirty?
FIONA: Maybe.
VARI: Go on.
FIONA: I'm going to get pregnant.
VARI: You are not.
FIONA: I am so.
VARI: You can't.
FIONA: Wait and see.
VARI: Is that the joke?
FIONA: It'll stop her.
VARI: How will it?
FIONA: She can't go and leave me with a baby. I'm 15. What
  would people say? She'd care about that though she doesn't
  give a shit about me.
VARI: You'll wreck your life.
FIONA: No, I won't.
VARI: Who's going to do it?
FIONA: Ewan Campbell. Do you mind?
VARI: Does he? Do you fancy him?
FIONA: He's all right.
VARI: Why don't you come and stay with us?
FIONA: Your mum's a bitch.
VARI: She's two-faced. She'd only be nasty behind your back.
  You can't sleep with someone you just think's all right.
FIONA: I thought you'd think it was a good idea.
VARI: It's a terrible idea.
FIONA: You've gone with him.

40

VARI: I'm a virgin and that's the way I'm going to stay till I get
     married which I'll do when I'm 26 and have three very
     quick children and be back to work 'cause I'm not going to
     be a skivvy like my mum. My man'll have enough money to
     buy a woman to do for me and private nurseries.
FIONA: What's the point in having them then?
VARI: You've got to have babies.
FIONA: Right.
VARI: Not when you're 15.
FIONA: Watch me. I'll be here on Saturday night after the film.
     It's the right time in my menstrual cycle. I'll get pregnant.
VARI: You know an awful lot suddenly.
FIONA: I've been to the library.
VARI: You've not to do it.
FIONA: She'll bloody stay. I won't live on my own. She'll bloody
     stay.

1983
The beach.
MORAG: (*From above*) I've brought ice-cream cones. You can't
     have a holiday without ice-cream cones. Where are your
     three lovely children?
VARI: My mum takes them for a morning sometimes.
MORAG: That'll give you a wee break. She'll be very proud of
     you, your mum.
VARI: Sorry?
MORAG: Your big house and your fine doctor husband.
VARI: She thinks I'm mad.
MORAG: Why is that, dear?
VARI: I went in for Shona, my third. I told her. She didn't
     speak to me for six months. Said if I wanted to ruin my life
     it was my affair.
MORAG: I see.
VARI: Look at me. I'm fat. I've seen you, Fiona. You can't keep
     your eyes off my tummy. I strip myself at night. He's not
     often there so no one sees. I look at myself in the mirror.
     This is a mother's body. Where am I? Don't think I pity
     myself. I wanted this from when I was wee. I'm feeling

41

puzzled. Where am I? My tits have got great blue veins running across them. They look good when they're full of milk but then it's mostly running down my front so the effect's somewhat spoilt. When they're empty they're poor things. All the exercises in the world'll not save my stomach. The doctor's face when I'd had Moira. He pulled out a handful of skin. I said that'll go away won't it. He let it go. Splat. He shook his head. He looked awful sad. He probably knows Archie. Felt sorry he had to make love to a doughbag for the rest of his life. I mean, I could have an operation. Archie's said already about it. They take away all the stretched-out skin. You end up looking like a hot cross bun. They cut you from here to here and up. I'd rather buy a corset. I mean, God or no God, you're asking for it if you fiddle. I mean, I'm healthy. You can have it on the National Health, the operation. Archie wouldn't compromise his principles even for the sake of his own pleasure. There's always divorce.

MORAG: What God's intended God's appointed.

FIONA: Don't say that.

VARI: Listen, it's easier if he's not there. I can handle the children. I eat what they eat. We get on fine. When he's in he enquires politely about the mess, makes requests about the level of the noise and I have to cook him dinner. It's not his fault. He's got his work. He likes a cooked breakfast too. Archie's very good to me. He lets the babies sleep in the bed with me and he goes to another room. We're lucky we have a good big house. That way he gets his sleep and I only have to turn over when they wake in the night. Of course we don't make love but I wake up covered in milk and piss, I can do without sperm as well. I beg your pardon, Auntie Morag.

FIONA: Do you miss sex?

VARI: I've read every book in existence on the female orgasm. I've never had one.

MORAG: Still. We'll get into heaven. (*Pause.*) You're very quiet, Fiona. (*Pause.*) Though you're my own daughter and I love you, I have to say it. You were always common.

42

(MORAG *throws a travelling rug round her shoulders and slowly leaves.* VARI *and* FIONA *sit in the gloaming of evening.*)

1966
The beach.
EWAN *comes in through the tunnel.*
EWAN: Where are you? Stop playing bloody silly games.
FIONA: I'm here.
(VARI *moves into the shadows.*)
EWAN: Where did you get the towel?
FIONA: I left it here this afternoon.
EWAN: It'll be damp.
FIONA: The rocks keep their heat.
EWAN: What number do you go to?
FIONA: I go up to ten and back again.
EWAN: Christ.
FIONA: It's your lucky night.
EWAN: Are you serious?
FIONA: Yes.
EWAN: I haven't got a thing.
FIONA: What?
EWAN: French letter.
FIONA: Never mind.
EWAN: Are you kidding me?
FIONA: No.
EWAN: You're not one of them?
FIONA: What?
EWAN: They're low.
FIONA: Who?
EWAN: PTs
FIONA: No.
EWAN: You're not a virgin then?
FIONA: Do you want to do it?
EWAN: I think so.
FIONA: Make up your mind.
EWAN: I'm surprised.
FIONA: Have you done it before?
EWAN: I've gone quite far.

43

FIONA: Right then.

EWAN: What?

FIONA: Let's start.

EWAN: Are you sure it's safe?

FIONA: Do you want to or not?

EWAN: Are you going to take your clothes off?

FIONA: It's not that warm.

EWAN: You don't sound very excited.

FIONA: Neither do you.

EWAN: It takes a bit of getting used to.

FIONA: You do fancy me?

EWAN: Yes. Yes, of course I do.

FIONA: Do you think I'm cheap for wanting to do it?

EWAN: I respect you.

FIONA: Right then. We could kiss first.

EWAN: Yes, of course.

(VARI *creeps up as they kiss*.)

VARI: That doesn't look very exciting.

FIONA: It's not.

VARI: Better do something.

FIONA: What?

VARI: Bite his ear.

FIONA: That's not very original.

VARI: Just do it.

(FIONA *bites* EWAN's *ear*.)

His hand moved. Stick your tongue in.

FIONA: Where?

VARI: His ear, stupid. Go on.

(FIONA *does as she's told*.)

Has he got a hard-on?

FIONA: I don't know.

VARI: Find out.

FIONA: How?

VARI: Do you want me to do it for you?

FIONA: No.

VARI: Stick your hand on it.

(FIONA *does*.)

Don't be so rough. Is it hard?

FIONA: I think so.

VARI: Lie down.

FIONA: Where?

VARI: On your back.

FIONA: I haven't any knickers on. Do you think he'll get a fright?

VARI: How do I know?

FIONA: You practically did it with him.

VARI: What did you take your knickers off for?

FIONA: I thought they'd get in the way.

VARI: He's puffing a bit. His hand's moved right up your leg.

FIONA: This is quite exciting.

VARI: Lie down quick.

(FIONA *moves away from* EWAN *and lies on the towel*.)

FIONA: He hasn't touched my tit yet. He should, shouldn't he?

VARI: It's not compulsory.

FIONA: I thought you had to.

VARI: Considering what you're offering a tit's a bit tame.

(EWAN *moves on top of* FIONA.)

FIONA: Is this it?

VARI: Has he got it out?

FIONA: I don't know.

VARI: You must know.

FIONA: What if he comes before it's in?

VARI: I don't know. Do you like it?

FIONA: Yes. Ouch.

VARI: What?

FIONA: It's in.

VARI: You're dirty.

FIONA: You can go.

(VARI *goes*.)

EWAN: You were a virgin.

FIONA: So were you.

EWAN: You must love me an awful lot.

FIONA: Do you want to do it again?

EWAN: Why?

FIONA: Didn't you like it?

EWAN: Yes, but . . .

FIONA: What?

EWAN: Did you?

FIONA: Yes. Well. Very nearly.

EWAN: You're not supposed to, are you?

FIONA: Why not?

EWAN: You're female. Whores enjoy it.

FIONA: Are you saying I'm a whore?

EWAN: I don't know, do I?

FIONA: I was a virgin.

EWAN: Do you love me?

FIONA: No, I don't.

EWAN: What did you do it for then?

FIONA: You're not to tell anyone.

EWAN: I won't.

FIONA: If I hear you've told; if I hear a word about this night on the beach, I'll say you couldn't do it.

EWAN: I thought it would be different. (*Pause*.) Are you angry with me?

FIONA: You're the only other one here.

EWAN: What did you do it for?

FIONA: You did it too.

EWAN: Will I see you again?

FIONA: I'll be getting the bus on Monday morning.

EWAN: I mean see you.

FIONA: I know fine what you mean.

EWAN: Well?

FIONA: Go home, Ewan.

EWAN: I promised your mum I'd see you safe to your front door.

FIONA: What could happen to me?

EWAN: You know.

FIONA: Tell me.

EWAN: What's up with you?

FIONA: Tell me.

EWAN: Rape. Fiona. I could give you a cuddle.

FIONA: Och, Ewan, it'll not fix itself. Go away and leave me alone.

EWAN: Come here.

46

FIONA: Just go away, will you. Please.

EWAN: I'll see you on Monday morning.

FIONA: I do like you.

(EWAN *goes through the tunnel*.)

VARI: So. Now we wait.

FIONA: Och, shut up.

(VARI *goes, singing 'Bye, Bye, Blackbird'*. FIONA *stays on the beach and joins in for two or three verses*.)

All right. I've made a mistake. I won't get pregnant. I won't get pregnant. I bet I won't. I bet I won't. Virgins don't very often get pregnant first off. It'll be tonight. That'll be the end of it and I won't speak to him again. He can be at the bus stop all he likes, I won't so much as look at him. Stuck-up pig. Who does he think he is, with his great long legs and his manners? Stuff his manners. Stuff him. I mean, it takes two. He didn't have to. He could have said no. Stupid black PVC raincoat. He thinks he's great. He's not, he's not. I'll swim in the sea. I'll wash him all off me. He'll be nowhere. I'll wash him all out of me. He won't exist. He won't be in me. He'll be in his stupid piece of black plastic and nowhere else. I'll be clear. I'm so cold.

MORAG: Fiona. What are you doing?

FIONA: Nothing.

MORAG: Are you all right?

FIONA: I'm fine.

MORAG: Do you know what the time is?

FIONA: Late.

MORAG: You shouldn't be on the rocks at this hour. You should have come straight home after the pictures. I've sat up waiting.

FIONA: Come for a swim.

MORAG: What's the matter with you?

FIONA: I feel like a swim.

MORAG: It's the middle of the night.

FIONA: Best time.

MORAG: It's cold.

FIONA: Keep your clothes on.

MORAG: All right.

FIONA: You're kidding.

MORAG: In, under and out. Race you.

FIONA: You're kidding.

MORAG: Race you. Come on.

FIONA: You're mad. It's bloody freezing in there.

MORAG: It's your idea.

FIONA: You're on.

MORAG: On your marks, get set, go.

(*They rush in.*)

Oh, my God.

FIONA: Jesus Christ.

MORAG: Beat you.

FIONA: It's a draw.

MORAG: I got in first.

FIONA: I was under first.

MORAG: Last one out's a cissy.

FIONA: Ready, steady, go.

(*They race out on to the rocks.*)

Jesus.

MORAG: Come here and give me a cuddle.

(*They put their arms round each other.*)

What happened?

FIONA: When?

MORAG: You were upset.

FIONA: I'm bloody freezing.

MORAG: We'll have a mug of hot chocolate when we get in.

FIONA: Me for the bath first.

MORAG: Was it wandering hands?

FIONA: Yes.

MORAG: You just have to be firm.

FIONA: I was.

MORAG: That's all right then.

FIONA: Mum . . .

MORAG: What?

FIONA: Race you to the house.

(*Blackout.*)

SCENE 2

1983
The beach. The sun is shining.
FIONA *is sitting with a towel round her shoulders.* VARI *is on the travelling rug.*

VARI: Do you find it much changed?

FIONA: It's the same.

VARI: You're not looking. See round the corner. There's a nuclear power station.

FIONA: Where?

VARI: Breathe in. Go on. Through your nose. What do you smell?

FIONA: Air.

VARI: There you are, you see. No sewers. You can't smell the shit, can you?

FIONA: Where is it? This nuclear power station.

VARI: It's like a fairy palace when it's all lit up.

FIONA: You like it.

VARI: Away back there. The sun shines off the sea and the glass of the reactors. It's a jewel in the green trees.

FIONA: Don't be daft.

VARI: There's building dirt from the B reactor. That's begun now. Do you know what they're doing with the dirt? Do you?

FIONA: Tell me.

VARI: Land from the sea. They're reclaiming it. See, that's creative. That shows conscience. And the work isn't allowed to disturb the environment. On that site there's flowers and trees. That's considerate. They fixed the sewers.

FIONA: You live round the corner from that.

VARI: I'm not the only one.

FIONA: Come on.

VARI: Lots of people do.

49

FIONA: For Christ's sake.

VARI: It's clean. It's awful pretty. All those lights twinkling like stars in the black night.

FIONA: Waste.

VARI: My mother always said it doesn't matter what the house is like, it can be a midden as long as the bathroom's clean. Then you know the woman of the house hasn't been got by the Apathy. I mean this place. It was a shit bin. I've three children. Shit can kill. Dog shit. People shit. My children wouldn't have been allowed near this beach if the sewers hadn't been fixed. Because they might tire me out but I love them.

FIONA: It wasn't as bad as that.

VARI: Wasn't it?

FIONA: How many reactors are there going to be?

VARI: A, B and C. You haven't kids, what do you know? You were never a mother.

FIONA: What was I then?

VARI: Down the road the old coal-fired place belting its muck out. Remember? Wind off the sea, shit; wind from the West, smoke. It's shut down now. Breathing that stuff. You don't live here. I mean, having the baby, it was a hiccup for you. You dropped it, passed it on, gave it away. You know nothing. It had no effect on your life. You changed schools. You got to university. Look at you now. No responsibilities. What do you know? It was all taken care of for you.

FIONA: I was 15.

VARI: I'm 32. Sometimes I feel 50. You got away with it. Slender young thing. I hate you.

FIONA: If there's an accident with the reactors your kids will suffer.

VARI: See, you. You've changed. You've got thinner. Me, I'm always going to be lumpy. So I hate you. Your face is taut, you've got cheek-bones. You've got the make-up right in the corner of your eyes. That takes time. I haven't got time. You'll be a member of CND and some left-wing political group with militant affiliations and pacifist intent.

You'll wear dungarees, speak harsh words of men and belong to a feminist encounter group where you look up your genitals with a mirror. I watch telly. Of course your blouses come from market stalls ten a penny but your shoes cost a packet. I know you. I've seen you on demonstrations on the telly. I haven't got time. I keep my hair short for it's less bother that way. I wear a pair of elastic panties from Marks and Spencers to keep my tummy in and to stop my bum from shoogling. I play badminton once a week in the same church hall we had the youth club in when we were young and I promise myself I'll have a sauna in some health club and a weekend in London when my youngest is weaned. If Archie says I can. For he's got the money. I have acquired a major accomplishment. Compromise. Listen. This is what I chose. I'm happy till you march in with no bottom and a social conscience.

FIONA: I'm sorry.

VARI: What for? You can't help it any more than I can. But get it right, Fiona, get it right.

(VARI *wanders down and stands looking out to sea*.)

1966
The beach.

FIONA: (*Very quickly*) Last week, I was on the bus, upstairs. I was going to see Dorothy and this girl up the front, she started having a fit or something. Must have been the heat. There were lots of people there between her and me but they, none of them . . . I went over to her and did what I could. She was heavy. I'd heard about them biting through their tongues. Epileptics. It wasn't pretty. Me and this other bloke took her to the hospital. But I saw her first. He wouldn't have done anything if I hadn't. I didn't get to see Dorothy. Well? That's worth something, isn't it? God. Are you listening? I'm not trying to bribe you. It's plain economics. I mean, I've made a mistake. It was my fault and I was wrong. I take it all on me. OK. Now if you let it make me pregnant . . . God. Listen, will you. If I'm pregnant it'll ruin four people's lives. Five. Right? My

51

mum'll be disappointed and her man'll walk out on her. That's two. Are you with me, God? I'll not be very happy. My mother'll hate me for the rest of my life for what I've done and that's not easy to live with. That's three. I'm still counting, God. Ewan'll be in for it. Well, he can't avoid it. I'm illegal and I've never been out with anybody else. Not that nobody fancied me. I wouldn't like you to think I was unpopular. Lots of people fancied me. My mum said I had to wait till I was 16. Then she relented just when Ewan happened to be there. Poor old Ewan. That's four, God, that's four. Then there's the baby. If it's there and if I have it it's got no chance. It would be born in Scotland. Still there, are you? I hate Scotland. I mean, look at me. If I have an abortion the baby'll be dead so that'll be five anyway.

VARI: Who the hell are you talking to?

FIONA: 'scuse me. Cover your ears.

VARI: Eh?

FIONA: Do it. This is private. Thank you. Sorry, God. You'll see from the aforegoing that you really don't need another soul in the world through me. You could let my mum have a miracle baby with her man. She's only 42. It's still possible and she'd be really chuffed if you would. So we'll regard that as settled then. Thank you very much for your attention. You can deal with something else now. Amen.

VARI: There's no God.

FIONA: I know.

VARI: What are you doing then?

FIONA: You were listening.

VARI: What do you expect? How are you feeling?

FIONA: Fine, thanks. How are you?

VARI: You know what I mean.

FIONA: The fair on Saturday. Did you go? I stayed on the chairoplanes for half an hour. It cost me a fortune. I was sick when I got off.

VARI: What for?

FIONA: I thought I might shake it loose.

VARI: You think it's there then?

FIONA: I don't know.

VARI: When are you due?

FIONA: Next week.

VARI: I can't stand the suspense. It's making me itchy.

FIONA: Look. It's my mum.

(MORAG *is above*.)

VARI: So what?

FIONA: You're not to say anything.

MORAG: Dinner's ready.

FIONA: Can Vari come? Will there be enough food?

VARI: I've got my dinner waiting for me at home.

MORAG: My man'll be there.

FIONA: That'll be nice. You're coming.

VARI: Don't order me about.

FIONA: Please.

VARI: I'll have to phone my mum.

(*Blackout*.)

1966
The beach.
FIONA *is alone on the beach in the sunshine.*

FIONA: Three old ladies with shopping bags. God. One blind
woman to the hairdresser's. That was a hard one. It was right
out of my way. How many stars do I get for that? I mean, do
you deal in stars as well as black marks? God. Here's the
biggie. I fixed it for my mum to go with her man. I don't
want to be left. You've got to realize I've made a big sacrifice.
I've been completely unselfish. How many people can come
here and say that to you, God? I've done something entirely
for someone else. Are you impressed? Are you? I've fixed it
for my mum to go to the Trucial States with her man. His
name's Robert, just so you know. I'm going to go to Vari's.
You really should do something about her mother. Talk
about black marks. So it's fixed. Were you around when I
did it? It was at the dinner table. He was there, Robert, and
so was Vari. I said, 'By the way. I think you two need to be
alone together for the start of your marriage. Why don't you
take your honeymoon on the Gulf? I'll be very happy to stay
with Vari and I hope you two'll be happy for you have my
blessing.' I did it just like that. Sort of formal and casual at
the same time. The right touch, I thought. Vari giggled. My
mum. Did you see? My mum lit up. I've never seen her look
like that. She's always had these graven lines from her nose
to her mouth. Way since I can remember. They went. Daft,
eh, God? Bet you weren't looking. I've never seen anyone
look happy like that. He, Robert, looked more than a wee bit
pleased too. I don't want her to go. I'll have nobody it doesn't
matter with. I won't have somebody of my own. I'll have to
write letters. I hate writing letters. Still, I think it's worth it.
Don't you, God? They say I can go out for the school
holidays. I'll like that fine. Listen to me, God. You've not to

54

let those little fish meet the seed. Let them chase their own tails. Anything you like. Kill them off. Don't let them make a baby. God. God. Are you there? God. Come on. Och, damn you then.

(EWAN *comes down through the tunnel on to the rocks.*)

EWAN: Hello.

FIONA: Hello.

EWAN: How have you been?

FIONA: Fine.

EWAN: I've not seen you at the bus stop.

FIONA: I've been getting the 42.

EWAN: I see.

　　(*Pause.*)

FIONA: How have you been?

EWAN: Very well, thank you.

FIONA: And your studies?

EWAN: Fine. What about you?

FIONA: Prime university material.

EWAN: That's good then.

FIONA: Yes. (*Pause.*) You don't have to be polite because we've fucked.

　　(*Pause.*)

EWAN: I hear your mother's going away.

FIONA: That's the idea.

EWAN: When?

FIONA: It'll be a couple of months yet. (*Pause.*) Did you know that the moment of conception can take place up to two days after a fuck? I mean, you don't just do it and boom you're pregnant. It can take up to two days of swimming. I wonder what I was doing when I conceived.

EWAN: I don't . . .

FIONA: I could have been having a piss at the time or playing netball. I've been playing a lot of netball and badminton and tennis. I've been swimming. Hockey's over but I've been playing volleyball. Two a side. It's a fast game. I've fallen over a lot. Look at this knee. It's had a terrible thumping. We won the school badminton tournament, me and my partner. We were rank outsiders. A hundred-to-one shot. I could have been playing badminton when I conceived. My O levels start next week.

EWAN: Are you pregnant by me?

FIONA: That was the idea.

EWAN: Why?

FIONA: I love you madly and I want to be your wife.

EWAN: Will you marry me?

FIONA: Very noble.

EWAN: Well?

FIONA: How old are you?

EWAN: Seventeen next month.

FIONA: I'm 15. I don't want to marry you. I don't want to marry anyone and I don't want to have a baby.

EWAN: Don't you like me?

FIONA: Not much. I'm sure you're a very nice person but you're not really my type.
(*Pause.*)

EWAN: You're being honourable.

FIONA: No.

EWAN: You couldn't have done it with me if you hadn't loved me.

FIONA: It was quite exciting.
(*Pause.*)

EWAN: What are we going to do?

FIONA: It's nothing to do with you.

EWAN: It's my child.

FIONA: You were the donor. That's all. You're not to tell anyone. I'm doing my O levels in peace.

EWAN: Will you get rid of it?

FIONA: Probably. Now go away.
(*He gets up to go.*)
Ewan. Do you love me?

EWAN: I could get used to the idea.

FIONA: If you didn't love me why did you do it? Promise you won't tell.
(EWAN *goes through the tunnel.*)
I wasn't christened. That's what's wrong, isn't it? I was a lost soul to begin with. I'll get christened if you'll take it

away. Do me a favour, will you, God. It's not my fault I wasn't christened. I feel sick all the time and I've got to get through my O levels. Churches make me cry. I'll believe in you if you'll take this away. I don't like it at all.

(VARI *enters*.)

VARI: You're getting fat.

FIONA: I know.

VARI: You'll have to tell. Your mum's going in a fortnight.

FIONA: She's sold the house.

VARI: You shouldn't have let her do that. What does it feel like?

FIONA: Heavy. I'm tired all the time.

VARI: Isn't it nice?

FIONA: No.

VARI: I think you're lucky. You'll never be alone again.

(MORAG *comes through the tunnel*.)

FIONA: Shut up. Jesus, that's stupid.

MORAG: I've bought so many things. Fiona, I bought you two dresses. I took a guess at the size. You're chubby these days but awful pretty. Take them back if you don't like them. Vari, I've bought you a jumper. You've a nice bust. It's a skinny rib. Here. It'll show you off. You mind with the boys now. Fiona, I've one for you too. You're getting a bust yourself. Think yourself lucky. I've done without all my life. That'll be your father's side of the family.

VARI: You shouldn't have bought anything for me, Auntie Morag.

MORAG: Don't you like it?

VARI: It's lovely. Thank you very much.

MORAG: Fiona?

FIONA: It's smashing.

MORAG: I wish you both health to wear them.

VARI: And happiness.

MORAG: You'll have that, all right. You're fair good girls.

FIONA: OK, God. I'm not going to tell her. This is what I've decided. You're to back me up now, you hear. I'll do it on my own. After she's gone. After the O levels, I'll go down to London and get an abortion and don't you come it. You've left me no choice. I mean, it wasn't much to ask.

57

She'll leave me money. She's bound to. Vari and me'll say we're going to visit friends. Kate Alex, her that had the restaurant, she moved to London. She'll back us. All you've got to do. Are you listening? Don't let me down this time. All you've got to do is not let me show till after she's gone and the O levels are past. I mean, chubby's all right but I don't want any bumps. Now listen to me. You've done nothing I've asked so far. Don't go trying anything off your own bat. I've taken the initiative. No bumps. Right? Right, God? Right?

MORAG: Fiona.

FIONA: What?

(*Silence.* FIONA *and* MORAG *look at each other.*)

Hey, God.

(*Silence.*)

1966

The beach.

EWAN *is at the tunnel entrance.* FIONA *walks over to him.*

FIONA: You're a wee shit, aren't you?

EWAN: I did it for the best.

FIONA: What best? Who's best? What were you? Playing the fucking hero. Is that it?

EWAN: I hardly think . . .

FIONA: No, you don't, do you? You don't think. What did you think was gonnie happen? Come on. I'm interested. What did you think you'd accomplish with your blabbing mouth? What did you think? What did you think? I'm fucking fascinated to know.

EWAN: I thought . . .

FIONA: I can see you, standing there with your head bowed. Did you bow your wee head, Ewan, in all humility: Did you duck your wee fat bonce? Were your big bony knees shaking? Were you humble? 'I'm awfully sorry, Mrs McBridie, but your dear sweet daughter Fiona, of whom I'm awfully fond, I hope you'll forgive me but I stuck one up her and now she's in the family way.' Is that your style, Ewan? Is it? Did it go like that?

Did I get it right? Answer me.

EWAN: I think . . .

FIONA: No, not you. Did you come the big man? Did you stand there tall, your proud head held high? Up on your high arse. 'I've done wrong, Mrs McBridie. Fiona's pregnant. I have no apologies to make. I'm prepared to marry her.' Was that it, Ewan? Or did you tell her her daughter's a whore? Did you sit her down with a nice wee drink? Did you bring her a bunch of flowers? Did you walk her round the garden? How did you tell her? Come on. Come on. Answer me. Cunt.

(EWAN *hits Fiona. Silence.*)

That's a mighty answer. There's a big man. Potent and virile. He can fuck a bint and he can swing his fists too.

EWAN: It wasn't easy.

FIONA: No.

EWAN: I felt I had to.

FIONA: Yes.

EWAN: You couldn't go on alone.

FIONA: What do you think I'm going to be now? I was getting on fine with my mother and she liked me. We were turning into good companions. What do you think you've done to that?

EWAN: You're pregnant.

FIONA: Congratulations.

EWAN: Fiona.

FIONA: Och, well.

EWAN: I felt I had to.

FIONA: Go away.

EWAN: I . . .

FIONA: Go away.

(EWAN *goes out.* FIONA *sits on the towel.*)

1983

The beach.

MORAG: We've had beautiful weather. We've been that lucky with the weather. Of course, we were always tanned when we lived here. In the summer months. Now they're saying

59

it's not good for you, the sun. I can't see that that's right.
I mean too much of anything . . . Look at orange juice
and that man. Or was it carrots that killed him? But that
was plain silly. Sun. In this country. How can you get too
much? And they made that pool with their own hands.
Men. They brought their wee tools and they chiselled it
out in the hot days. Drinking their beer and telling their
dirty jokes. Well, they would, wouldn't they? Men do.
They built it to save their feet on the hot rocks. Great soft
things. Fancy going to all that trouble to save a
fifteen-yard walk. They never brought their wives. Of
course, that was when I was wee. When I think of it now,
I think they must have been the unemployed. They were
here an awful lot. Nice men they were too. They got
raucous as the day went on with the beer and then I
wasn't allowed near the beach. The storms there were.
Summer and winter. You'd see the spray coming right up
over the roofs of the houses. I used to stand in the mouth
of the tunnel. I used to dare the waves to come and get
me. I'd run forward and I'd run back. My mum'd leather
me for being wet when I got in. It was worth it. Once I
asked her for a raincoat. A special present for my
birthday. A real waterproof. I wanted it to keep me dry
from the spray. She bought it for me. It was a real one.
Kept me snug and dry. When I got in my mum belted me
across the face. She had a hard hand. Then she chased me
round the house with the bread knife. For getting the
raincoat wet. She was angry. I feel so disappointed.

FIONA: We could have gone to the Lakes for Christ's sake.
MORAG: I'll love you whatever you do. You know that. I've
    loved you through it all.
FIONA: Don't be stupid.
MORAG: You're my daughter.
FIONA: If I tortured, if I murdered, you'd love me then?
MORAG: You're my flesh and blood.
FIONA: It means nothing. (*She clicks her fingers.*) It means *that*.
    It's an insult, Mother.
MORAG: I stood by you.

FIONA: Is that why we've come here?

MORAG: I wanted to talk. I couldn't talk to you. You're a queer lass but I love you.

FIONA: Did it ever occur to you, you had a choice?

MORAG: What?

FIONA: You had a choice. Did you know that? Did you know you had a choice?

MORAG: Suppose I did?

FIONA: Oh, Jesus.

MORAG: Further and further away from me. The years pass. Each day. Vegetarian food. Symphonies. You put up barriers and I'm . . . We never had a symphony in the house. There was no need. I mean, I had other things . . . Time was, I'd go out, I'd buy you something. Impulse. I'd be in a shop. Some wee thing. You'd like it. I'd know you'd like it. Now. I wanted to talk to you. Books. I don't like Dickens. I never did. I like Georgette Heyer and I like the television. I'm very fond of the television. Your flat. You've not got an ashtray in your flat. Not a single one.

FIONA: I don't smoke. (Repeat with new Morag.)

Change Morag here

MORAG: Of course you don't smoke. Live and let live. I've always said that. I hold to that. You have men and I say nothing though I'd like it if you'd talk to me. For years I held down a good job.

FIONA: I know you did.

MORAG: I'm not a stupid woman.

FIONA: I never said . . .

MORAG: Choice, choice, choice. Yes, yes. I knew there was a choice. Let me find the right word. I like to have the right word. The exact right word. Culpable. You and me. See now. I know you're not all to blame. I'm culpable. Not the going away.

FIONA: What then?

MORAG: I mean, I met a man and I loved him. I met a man and I was glad he wanted me. Do you see? I wanted to go away with him. So what's more natural than that? Come on.

FIONA: I told you to . . .

61

MORAG: See me now. Look. I knew what I'd become. I made a break for something. OK. When he came to me, Ewan. When he came to me and told me.

FIONA: Mum, this is . . .

MORAG: You listen. 'Mrs McBridie, Fiona's going to have a child. It's my child. I'm sorry, Mrs McBridie.' Oh, he was polite. I liked him. Poor wee fella. I liked him fine.

FIONA: He was . . .

MORAG: Now listen to me. I knew I had a choice. Listen. My daughter had not come to me. Do you understand that? My daughter was not asking for my help. I could see her point. Listen. I had a choice. What if I left her enough money and I went away? Nothing mentioned between us. I knew you'd not have that child. Then you might say we'd survive, you and me. Out of the question. Fifteen and pregnant. Of course I couldn't let you alone. So. You told Ewan. So. Here we both are. Here we are. (*Pause.*) I expect you'd like an ice-cream cone. I'll walk up the prom a bit. My last walk of this holiday. I don't expect you ever will talk to me. Would you like a double 99 with raspberry sauce? That's what I'm having. My own wee treat. Will you join me? You've got to do something daft on a last day.

FIONA: That would be lovely.

MORAG: Don't if you'd rather not.

FIONA: Bunny rabbit's ears. A double 99.

MORAG: You'll join me then?

FIONA: Yes.

MORAG: After all, it's not meat.

FIONA: I'll join you.

MORAG: That's good then. That's very good.

(*She goes off up the tunnel.* VARI'*s voice comes from beside the swimming pool.*)

VARI: Your mother's alive. They all are, that generation. My mother's the same. She's an old cow but she's zinging with it. Life. Me, sometimes I get this awful dizzy feeling. I'm standing there. I'm doing something. I don't know what day of the week it is. I panic. I mean, I really don't know. I hang on to myself. If I don't I'll fall down. I put my arms

62

round myself and hug tight. I hug very tight. I look out the window to see what the weather's like. See, I don't know where I am in the year. And I'm dizzy. I lean my back to the sink. I check the big tree outside the window. If it's got leaves. I look down at my clothes. What's the month? What month is it? What year is it? How many children have I got? Am I pregnant now? Have I just given birth? I don't know. I don't know. And then it comes to me. It's Wednesday. It's October. It's Sunday. It's April. It's all the same and I turn back to the sink. I wash the nappies by hand. I've got a washing machine, don't you worry. One of the ones that does it all. You know, dries as well. I've a dish-washer too. I wash the nappies by hand. They're cleaner that way. Not that I care. I don't care, but you have to have something to talk about at mothers' mornings. Do something queer. Marks you out.

FIONA: My mother cares passionately about everything. Life and a ham sandwich. It all has the same importance. Not a touch of the Apathy. God? Do you still live here or have you moved on? Hung up your omniscience and retired the Recording Angel? Would it be too much to ask, I'd liked to be let alone?

(MORAG *comes through the tunnel with the ice-creams.*)

MORAG: Bunny rabbit's ears. The raspberry sauce is running down my hands. Here, take it quick, Fiona. I'd have brought you one, Vari, if I'd known. Here, have one of my ears.

VARI: Thank you, Auntie Morag.

MORAG: I've some whisky in my bag. Reach me it over. Our last day. You'll drink with us, the parting glass. Eat your ice-cream, Fiona. A wee bit of what you fancy.

(*She one-handedly arranges glasses and begins to unscrew the bottle as the lights fade down.*)